The Funny Girl

Raintree is an imprint of Capstone Global Library Limited, a company
incorporated in England and Wales having its registered office at 264 Banbury
Road, Oxford, OX2 7DY – Registered company number: 6695582

www.raintree.co.uk
myorders@raintree.co.uk

Text © Capstone Global Library Limited 2019
The moral rights of the proprietor have been asserted.

All rights reserved. No part of this publication may be reproduced in any
form or by any means (including photocopying or storing it in any medium by
electronic means and whether or not transiently or incidentally to some other
use of this publication) without the written permission of the copyright owner,
except in accordance with the provisions of the Copyright, Designs and Patents
Act 1988 or under the terms of a licence issued by the Copyright Licensing
Agency, Barnard's Inn, 86 Fetter Lane, London, EC4A 1EN (www.cla.co.uk).
Applications for the copyright owner's written permission should be addressed
to the publisher.

Designed by Hilary Wacholz
Original illustrations © Capstone Global Library Limited 2019
Originated by Capstone Global Library Ltd
Printed and bound in India

ISBN 978 1 4747 6198 7
22 21 20 19 18
10 9 8 7 6 5 4 3 2 1

British Library Cataloguing in Publication Data
A full catalogue record for this book is available from the British Library.

Waltham Forest Libraries	
904 000 00638466	
Askews & Holts	08-Feb-2019
STO	£5.99
5957337	

The Funny Girl

Something Smells Funny at the Talent Show

WRITTEN BY D.L. GREEN

ILLUSTRATED BY LEANDRA LA ROSA

raintree

a Capstone company — publishers for children

CONTENTS

HOMEWORK?
PASS.

When school started and Ms Fish started talking, I didn't pay much attention to her. I was busy finishing yesterday's homework. I had a very good reason for not finishing my homework last night: My second-favourite TV programme and my fifth-favourite TV programme had been on.

By the way, Ms Fish is not a fish. She is my teacher. I am not a fish either. I am a ten-year-old girl called Shelby Bloom. I live in Los Angeles with my parents, my older sister, my younger brother and my dog. My parents and my brother are annoying sometimes. My sister is annoying always. My dog is annoying only when he drools on me, but he can't help that.

As Ms Fish talked to the class, I worked on my maths homework, trying to work out 917 divided by 7. I wished I could use a calculator instead of going through a thousand long division steps.

Ms Fish talked and talked while I did my homework. Some of my classmates asked Ms Fish questions. I heard someone say, "When is it?" Another kid asked, "Is it just our class?" But I didn't pay much attention.

I had just worked out that 917 divided by 7 was 131, when I heard Ms Fish say, "Yes, there will be a prize."

Prize? I put down my pencil and stared at Ms Fish.

"The winner will get a homework pass," Ms Fish said.

"A homework pass!" I said.

"A homework pass!" a few other kids said.

Ms Fish nodded. "The winner will get to choose a day that he or she doesn't have to hand in homework."

I put up my hand and asked, "The winner of what? When? Where?"

"Shelby Bloom, you were not paying attention," my teacher said.

My friend Ajay Patel answered my questions. He said, "Ms Fish was talking about the winner of the talent show. The show will be in the assembly hall in two weeks. It's just for our class, and she's the judge."

"Thank you," I said. Ajay was a good friend.

"I am going to win the talent show," Brooke Crumpkin said.

Brooke was not a good friend. She was not even good. She was not even a friend. Actually, she was very mean. I did not want Brooke to win the talent show. What I really wanted was to win the talent show myself.

"*I* am going to win the talent show," I said.

"That's enough," Ms Fish said. "Everyone hand in your homework."

Ms Fish would not be happy when she saw my homework. I had only finished half of it.

My parents would not be happy either. Last time they found out I hadn't finished my homework, they made me stay at home all day on a Saturday. This time they would probably make me stay at home all weekend. I wouldn't be able to play basketball with Ajay or go horse riding or do any other fun things.

I wished I could get that homework pass right now. But even if I couldn't, I knew I'd have a good use for it.

To win the homework pass, I would have to:

1. Decide on a talent.

2. Create an act for the talent show.

3. Make sure I was better at my act than anyone else in the class.

That sounded really hard. But it was better than doing homework.

HAIR-FLAVOURED SNACKS

At break time I stood with some of my classmates at the edge of the playground. The temperature outside was about a thousand degrees, too hot to run around on the playground. So instead we watched some little kids on the jungle gym and ate snacks.

My dad had packed me a strawberry yoghurt today. It wasn't as good as the brownie he had packed for me yesterday, but it was better than the carrot sticks he had given me the day before.

Brooke walked up to us with her nose in the air. She said, "Don't waste your time practising for the talent show. I am going to win it."

"You can't win a talent show if you don't have any talent," I said.

Brooke sneered at me. *"You* can't win a talent show if *you* don't have any talent."

"You certainly don't have any talent for clever comebacks," I said.

"Yes I do," she said.

"'Yes I do' is not a clever comeback," I said.

"Hmmph," Brooke said.

"'Hmmph' also is not a clever comeback," I said.

She raised her nose in the air again like a snob and flicked her long hair.

That was not a clever comeback either.

Ajay said, "Your hair just got in my cherry yoghurt."

"Yuck." Latasha Kennedy frowned.

"Gross." Alice Nolan frowned.

"Brooke, you have a talent for getting your hair in people's food," I said. "But I don't think you'll win the talent show with that talent."

"I have many talents," she said. "My best talents are my gorgeous face, being tall and knowing about fashion."

I rolled my eyes. "Even if you had a gorgeous face, that's not a talent. Neither is being tall."

Brooke ignored me. "I will combine my talents for being gorgeous, tall and fashionable. I will model a fantastic outfit and win the talent show – and the homework pass."

I shook my head. "I am going to win the homework pass with my talent for telling jokes."

"You tell jokes, but you have no talent." Brooke flicked her hair again. This time it landed in my yoghurt.

"Yuck." Latasha frowned again.

"Gross." Alice Nolan frowned again too.

"You ruined my snack!" I threw the pot of ruined yoghurt into a nearby bin.

"You ruined my hair." Brooke strode away.

"I really want to win the homework pass," Ajay said. "I need to work on my act."

"What act?" I asked.

"I haven't quite decided on that yet," he said.

"What talents do you have?" I asked.

"I haven't quite decided on that yet either," he said.

"Good luck," I said. "But I hope I have better luck. I really want to win the talent show."

"I really want to win too. I'm a very talented gymnast," Latasha said. She performed a perfectly straight cartwheel right in front of us.

"I really want to win too. I'm a talented ballet dancer," Alice said. She raised her arms over her head, stood on her toes and twirled.

I would have some tough competition at the talent show.

"I really want to win too. I am really talented at yodelling," Will Carelli said. He cupped his hands over his mouth and yodelled. "Yodel – Ay – Eee – Oooo!"

I would also have some weak competition at the talent show.

IT'S NOT
FUNNY

At lunchtime I sat next to Rose Kowalski for four reasons:

1. She was my friend.

2. I wanted to practise my jokes for the talent show.

3. I was hoping she had brought her dad's delicious homemade cookies.

4. I was hoping she would share the cookies with me.

I asked Rose, "What do you need to get to high school?"

"Let's see," she said. She took a peanut butter and jam sandwich from her lunch box. "To get to high school, you need to have been through all the years at this school. You need to have taken some tests. And you need—"

"It's a joke," I said. "What do you need to get to high school?"

"A ladder," Rose said.

I frowned. "How did you know that joke?"

"You told it to me a while ago." Rose took a bag of carrot sticks from her lunch box.

"So if you hear a joke once, you don't think it's funny the second time?" I asked. I took a cheese sandwich out of a plastic bag and started eating.

Rose shrugged. "Your joke was really funny the first time. It was a bit funny the second time. Today is the third time I've heard the joke."

"Let me try one I've never told you before," I said as Rose bit into her sandwich. **"Knock, knock."**

"Who's there?" Rose asked. It sounded like "Who the?" because her mouth was full of sandwich.

"Ash," I said.

"Ash who? Gesundheit," she said. "I know that one too."

I sighed. "I don't remember telling you that joke."

"You didn't," Rose said. "You told Alice that one. Then she told me the joke the next day."

"I'm never going to win the talent show if most of the audience already knows my jokes," I said. "I really wanted the homework pass."

"It's not that big a deal," Rose said. "The homework pass is only for one day of homework. You still have to do homework all the other days."

"But I despise homework," I said. "One less day of homework is one less day of torture."

Rose reached into her lunch box again. She pulled out

a large chocolate chip cookie and said, "Maybe this will cheer you up."

I nodded. "It will. Thank you."

It did.

A few hours later, I decided to try out some jokes on my older sister, Lila, as we walked home from the bus stop after school. Lila was only a year older than me, but she was nothing like me. For instance, she loved to follow rules, which is why I called her Miss Priss. I liked to break rules, such as the rule about not calling people names.

I asked Lila, "What do you call an alligator in a vest?"

"Alligators don't wear vests," Lila said. "So you wouldn't call it anything."

"Huh?" I asked.

"You don't need a name for an alligator who wears a vest, because an alligator would never wear a vest," Lila said as we walked. "An alligator would bite anyone who tried to put a vest on it."

"It's a joke," I said.

"I don't get it," Lila said.

I sighed. "That's because I haven't told you the punch line. **What do you call an alligator in a vest?**"

Lila shrugged. "It depends on whether it's a boy alligator or a girl alligator. If it's a boy alligator in a vest, I'd call him Al, which is short for alligator. If it's a girl alligator in a vest, I'd call her Ally. Or Serena. I really like the name Serena."

We were almost home. Lila had been talking so much, I hadn't even finished telling one joke. **I finally said, "An alligator in a vest is called an investigator."**

Lila didn't laugh. Instead she asked, "Why? Does the alligator investigate crimes or something? Could you also call it a detective?"

I groaned. It was a good thing Lila wasn't judging the talent show, because I would never win.

My teacher was going to be the only judge. I hoped Ms Fish had a good sense of humour.

STILL NOT FUNNY

After school that day, I went into the kitchen for a snack. My mum and my little brother, Coop, were there. Mum was chopping fruit for a fruit salad. Coop was spinning in circles for no reason. He was four years old. He did a lot of crazy things for no reason. I stood a few steps away from him so he wouldn't spin into me.

"Do you know why the pony sounded strange?" I said. "Because he was a little hoarse."

Mum just kept slicing a banana.

"Don't you think that joke is funny?" I asked her.

"It was funny the first time you told it," Mum said.

"Where's the little pony?" Coop asked. "I want to ride the little pony."

"Sorry, Coop," I said. "It was just a joke."

I wondered whether a joke no one laughed at could still be called a joke. Probably not.

I tried again. "When do you put a tuba in the bathroom?"

"When it has to use the potty?" Coop asked.

"No," I said. "When it's a tuba toothpaste."

No one laughed. Mum finished cutting the banana. Coop stopped spinning and scratched his head.

"Shelby, you told me that joke before also," Mum said.

I sighed. "I'll try one more joke: Why are fish so clever?"

"Because they live in schools," Mum said.

I frowned. "I don't remember telling you that one."

"It's a really old joke. I heard it when I was a little girl," Mum said. "Do you want some fruit salad?"

"OK." I walked towards the bowl of fruit salad. On the way over, I slipped on a banana skin and fell to the floor.

Coop and Mum started laughing.

"*Now* you're laughing?" I asked. "Why are you laughing at me?"

Mum stopped laughing. She said, "Sorry, Shelby. When you slipped on the banana skin, I thought you were trying to be funny again. Are you OK?"

I stood and nodded.

"How much homework do you have?" Mum asked.

"Not much," I said.

Actually, I had a lot of homework. And I had to get it done, because I was starting to doubt whether my jokes could win the homework pass.

But first I decided to go across the street to Ajay's house. He loved good jokes. If he didn't laugh at my jokes, I would know I couldn't win the talent show.

WHAT'S THE POINT?

I walked across the street to try out some jokes on my neighbour Ajay.

He stood on his driveway. He kept dropping a basketball and picking it up, again and again. As I got closer to him, I saw that he was trying to spin the basketball on his pointer finger. But it wasn't working.

"Hey, Ajay." I joined him on his driveway. **"Did you hear about the dog who swallowed a firefly?"**

Ajay nodded. "The dog barked with de-light."

"Why aren't you laughing?" I asked.

"You told me that joke a while ago, when we were walking our dogs," Ajay said. "It's one of your best jokes."

"If it's one of my best jokes, then why didn't you laugh just now?" I asked.

Ajay dribbled the basketball. "Jokes aren't funny if you already know the punch line."

"Yes they are," I said.

"Did you hear about the dog who swallowed a firefly?" Ajay said. "It barked with de-light."

I crossed my arms. "Why are you repeating the joke I just told you?"

"To show you jokes aren't funny if you already know the punch line," Ajay said. "You didn't laugh after I repeated your joke."

"That's because you don't have my great comic timing," I said.

Ajay raised his eyebrows.

"OK. It's also because I already knew the punch line."
I sighed. "I wanted to use that joke in the talent show."

"I think you told that joke at break too," Ajay said.
"All the kids in our class who heard it will be in the
audience at the talent show. They won't laugh."

"Maybe I should slip on a banana skin to get some
laughs," I said.

"That's an old one," Ajay said. "No one with a good
sense of humour will laugh at that."

"My mum and my brother just did," I said.

"Oh." Ajay pointed his index finger skywards, placed
the basketball on top of it and gave the ball a quick spin.
An instant later, the spinning ball fell to the ground.

I picked it up. "Let's play basketball."

"I can't," Ajay said. "I have to practise my basketball
skills."

"What skills?" I joked.

Ajay finally laughed. "Spinning the ball on your finger
is a skill."

"It looks like you're not good at that skill," I said.

"I need to practise so I can do it at the talent show." Ajay placed the basketball on the tip of his pointer finger again and spun the ball. It quickly fell.

He tried again, this time spinning the ball before putting it on his finger. The ball fell just as quickly.

"You definitely need to practise," I said.

Ajay clutched the ball against his chest and said, "My favourite basketball player, Stephen Curry, can spin a basketball on his finger for a really long time. It looks so easy when he does it on TV."

"Maybe you should try a different basketball trick," I said.

"I'll try dribbling the ball behind my back," Ajay said. He dropped the basketball behind him. His arm flailed wildly. The ball bounced once behind Ajay's back, rolled down the driveway and landed in the gutter.

Ajay frowned. "That trick is also much harder than it looks on TV."

"Maybe a joke will cheer you up," I said. **"What did the triangle say to the basketball?"**

"You're pointless," Ajay said. "You told me that joke last week."

I shook my head. "No I didn't. Last week I said, 'What did the *rectangle* say to the basketball?'"

"It's the same punch line," Ajay said.

"Do you know what else is pointless?" I asked.

"A volleyball?" Ajay asked.

"It's pointless for either of us to try to win the talent show," I said. "No one is going to laugh at my old jokes. And dropping a basketball and picking it up a thousand times isn't really a talent."

"I'll try to find a different talent," Ajay said.

"Good idea." I nodded. But I didn't know if Ajay had any talents. He had a talent for being a nice friend, but I didn't see how he could perform niceness or friendship onstage.

"Shelby, why don't you find some new jokes for the talent show?" Ajay said.

"That sounds like a lot of work," I said.

"Do you know what else sounds like a lot of work?" he asked.

I frowned. "Homework. Work is even in its name."

Ajay laughed. "Good one. You can put that joke in your act."

"Thanks," I said. "Maybe preparing for the talent show won't be pointless after all."

WHAT'S IN MY EAR?

I sat with Rose the next day at lunch. Luckily, she had brought her dad's homemade cookies again. Even more luckily, Rose gave me a cookie.

I was just about to bite into it when Ajay came by. He sat across from us and asked, "Can I try out a magic trick on you?"

"OK," I said. **"Just don't make my cookie disappear."**

Rose and Ajay laughed. Then Ajay pointed to me and said, "Shelby, what's that in your ear?"

"Earwax? A family of fleas?" I joked.

"Gross," Rose said.

Ajay reached across the table and touched my ear. Then he said, "Abracadabra," put his fist on the lunch table, and opened it. There was a quarter on his palm. He said, "I magically found a quarter in your ear."

I grabbed it. "Thanks for returning it."

"Hey, that's mine," Ajay said.

"It's mine," I said. "You told me you found it in my ear."

"Finders, keepers," Ajay said. "Give me my quarter."

I returned his quarter and started eating my cookie. The cookie was a lot better than Ajay's magic trick. I didn't tell Ajay that.

"Do you think I can win the talent show with that magic trick?" Ajay asked.

"No," Rose said.

"Do you know any more magic tricks?" I asked.

Ajay shook his head. "I tried to learn other tricks, but they were too hard."

"I never heard of a magic show with just one trick." I frowned. I felt bad for Ajay and because I'd eaten my only cookie.

"Maybe I can do the same trick, but in different ways," Ajay said. "After I pull a quarter from your ear, I could pull a dime from another kid's ear and a nickel from someone else's ear."

"I don't think you'll win the talent show with that," I said. "It's still really only one trick."

Ajay sighed.

"Rose said we should stop worrying about winning the talent show," I said.

"Yeah," Rose said. "The homework pass is only for one day."

"I'll try not to worry," Ajay said.

The bell rang, and we walked back to class. Ms Fish

had written on the classroom whiteboard, "Research report due in two weeks."

I put up my hand. "What research report?"

"The big homework project I discussed before," Ms Fish said.

Oh. I must not have been paying attention. I was probably finishing a small homework project when Ms Fish was talking about the big homework project.

"We're supposed to research ten facts about a famous person," my friend Gabby Garcia whispered from the next table.

That sounded hard.

"And then use those facts to write a report," Gabby added.

That sounded horribly hard.

"I won't need to research facts or write a report," Brooke said. "I'm going to win the homework pass."

"*I'm* going to win it," I said.

But I wasn't sure I believed that.

TWO TERRIBLE SINGERS

My mum took me to the library after school. I borrowed three books:

A book called *500 New Jokes for Kids*

A book about how to tell jokes

A book about my favourite comedian, Tina Fey

As soon as I got home, I went to my room and closed my door. Then I sat on my bed and started reading the books and taking notes.

"Are you doing homework?" Mum asked from the other side of the door.

"Yes," I replied. I was at home, and I was doing work. I didn't tell Mum that I was preparing for the talent show.

I spent a long time choosing new jokes to tell at the talent show. I wrote them down neatly on the front and back of a piece of lined yellow paper.

I also read the book about telling jokes. It had a lot of good tips in it. For instance, it said to pause after every punch line, to give the audience time to laugh.

Then I read about how Tina Fey got to be so funny and famous. She had been my favourite comedian ever since I saw her film *Megamind*. She was also in *Muppets Most Wanted* and a few films for grown-ups that my gran and I had watched that we didn't tell my parents about. A good tip from the Tina Fey book was to let your personality shine onstage.

After I had written down the new jokes, I opened my

door and called Mugsy into my room. Mugsy is our huge, hairy mutt. He is the best dog ever.

He jumped on my bed, knocking my pillow to the floor and getting hairs all over my duvet. I gave him a hug and got hair all over my top and trousers. Then I stood next to the bed and practised my jokes on Mugsy.

Mugsy seemed to love my act. He stared at me and wagged his tail. He yapped happily after I told this joke: "I stayed up all night wondering where the sun was. Then it dawned on me."

After I told Mugsy the last joke on my list, Mum walked into my bedroom. She said, "I'm glad you're working so hard on your homework."

I didn't respond. I wasn't exactly doing homework. I wasn't *inexactly* doing it either. I wasn't doing it at all.

"It's almost dinner time," Mum said.

My stomach growled.

Mum laughed. "Good one! You're so funny."

"I didn't do that on purpose," I said.

"Oh. I thought you did." She shrugged. "I came in to tell you Ajay is at the front door."

I left Mugsy and Mum behind, went to the door and said hello.

Ajay took two steps forwards on our porch. Then he took two steps backwards. Then forwards, then backwards, and so on. While his feet stepped back and forth, his arms flapped up in the air and down to his sides, up and down, up and down, and so on.

"Are you OK?" I asked him. "Are you having a medical problem?"

He stopped moving his feet and flapping his arms. He said, "I was showing you my new talent."

"Talent for what?" I asked him. "Talent for acting like a confused bird?"

Ajay sighed. "It's a dance I made up. Maybe I should add some more moves."

I raised my eyebrows.

I thought he should subtract some moves. I thought he should subtract *all* the moves.

"I know I have talent buried somewhere," Ajay said.

I wished he'd bury his dance moves far below ground.

"It takes some people years to find their true talent," Ajay said. "My hero, Stephen Curry, didn't become a star basketball player until his second year of university."

Dad walked over to us from the kitchen. He sang in a screechy voice, "Come and eat! Have a treat! I like to rhyme! At dinner time!" That was my dad's annoying way of telling me it was time for dinner.

I sang, "I'll come along! If you stop that song!"

Dad laughed.

I frowned. My parents kept laughing at me when I didn't mean to be funny.

Ajay whispered to me, "Don't tell your dad, but he's not very talented."

I nodded. Dad's singing talent was about the same as Ajay's dancing talent: awful.

"Maybe I should sing while I dance," Ajay said.

"Or just sing and don't dance," I said.

Ajay started singing. It sounded more like screeching. "Ruuudolph the Red-Nosed Reindeeerrr." As he screeched, he did his confused bird dance again.

I tried not to make a face or cover my ears. Instead I said, "I have to go and have dinner now."

"What do you think is better?" Ajay asked. "My talent for singing or my talent for dancing?"

"They're both about the same," I said.

"Bye, Shelby," Ajay said. "I'm going home to work on my singing and dancing until they're good enough to win the talent show."

That would take forever.

During dinner Dad said, "I heard Ajay singing. Don't tell Ajay, but he's not very talented." Then Dad sang in his screechy voice, "Pass the peas! If you please! I already ate! The peas on my plate!"

Dad and Ajay both had a talent for being awful singers.

I had a talent for being funny. And now that I had a list of good, new jokes, I could win the talent show. I couldn't wait to get the homework pass! Goodbye, research report! Hello, more TV watching!

A PAPER BAG IS NOT A BASKETBALL PLAYER

The next morning, I put my list of jokes in my backpack and started walking to the bus stop with my sister, Lila. She wore a powder-blue blouse buttoned to her neck, a navy blue pleated skirt and a French plait that had taken her twenty minutes to make this morning. I wore a long red T-shirt and frayed jeans. As we walked, I stuffed my hair into a rubber band to make a ponytail.

"Wait for me!" Ajay shouted from across the street. He hurried over and walked with us.

Ajay pulled a brown paper bag out of his backpack and said, "Look what I made." He had used a marker pen to draw green eyes, a blue nose and a red mouth on the paper bag.

"Do you always draw on paper bags?" my sister asked him.

"It's not a paper bag," he said as we walked. "I mean, it *was* a paper bag. Now it's a puppet."

Ajay put his hand inside the paper bag and opened and shut it to make its red mouth move. "Hi, I'm Stephen," he said. His lips moved a bit as he spoke.

"What are you doing?" I asked.

"I'm doing my best talent yet. I'm a ventriloquist," he said. Then he opened and shut the paper bag's mouth again and mumbled, "I'm Stephen Curry." His mouth stayed closed, but his lips moved a lot.

"Stephen Curry the basketball player?" I asked.

"It looks like a paper bag to me," Lila said.

"It's Stephen Curry in puppet form," Ajay said. He flapped the paper bag open and closed again and said, with his mouth shut tight but his lips moving quite a bit, "Hi, I'm Stephen Curry. I like to dibble and duck."

"Dibble and duck?" I asked.

"Stephen was trying to say 'dribble and dunk'," Ajay said. "It's hard for him to talk clearly."

"You mean it's hard for *you* to talk clearly, Ajay," Lila said. Then she pointed to the puppet. "It still looks like a paper bag to me."

When we got to the bus stop, I pulled out my list of jokes and said, "I need to memorize my jokes for the talent show."

"First tell me what you think of my new talent," Ajay said.

"I'd hardly call it a talent." I shrugged. "Ventriloquists aren't supposed to move their mouths."

"Plus, they should be entertaining," Lila said. "It's not

very entertaining to watch a paper bag while you say, 'Hi, I'm Stephen Curry', and move your lips."

"True," I said.

"Shelby, you don't like any of my talents." Ajay frowned. "You don't like my basketball skills or my magic trick or my singing or dancing or puppetry."

"Just because you say you have a talent doesn't mean you really do," I replied.

Ajay returned his Stephen Curry paper bag to his backpack and said, "You're mean."

"I'm just being honest," I said. "You didn't laugh at my jokes when I told them to you."

"I laughed the first time you told them, even though some of them were never even funny the first time," Ajay said.

I glared at him.

As the bus pulled up, Ajay said, "I thought you were a nice friend. But you're not nice, and you're not a friend."

I put my hands on my hips. "Well, you're not talented."

"You're just jealous," Ajay said angrily.

"I am not jealous," I said just as angrily.

We got on the bus. For the first time in a long time, Ajay and I didn't sit together.

Fine. Who needed Ajay anyway? Not me. I had jokes to memorize and a talent show to win. I was sick of watching Ajay's bad attempts at talent.

I pulled out my list of jokes from my backpack. I stared at the list but couldn't focus. I kept reading the same joke over and over: *I wanted to be on time, so I sat on my watch*. Even though Ajay had nothing to do with being on time or watches, I kept thinking about him.

9

A TALENT FOR EVIL

After the bus dropped us off at school, Ajay and I walked in different directions without saying a word. I stopped at a tree near the entrance and leaned against it. It was a bright, sunny morning. But I didn't feel bright or sunny – more like dark and stormy.

I stared at my list of jokes again. But I still couldn't focus.

Brooke came up to me and said, "I bought the most amazing outfit to model at the talent show. I got a trendy dress, shiny tights and gorgeous boots. I'm going to describe every detail of my outfit at the talent show. Then I'll walk up and down a pretend runway."

"I think you'll win the talent contest," I said.

Brooke smiled.

"If your talent is putting people to sleep," I added. "Because it sounds really boring to hear you describe your clothes and watch you pace up and down."

Brooke rolled her eyes. "It's a lot more exciting than your old jokes. Everyone has heard them already. So they're not funny any more."

I waved my list of jokes at her. The yellow paper seemed as bright to me as the morning sunshine. I said, "I have a list of brand new, very funny jokes."

"Let me see your list," Brooke said.

"No way." I shook my head. "No one is going to hear

any of these jokes until the talent show. Then they'll laugh so hard. That homework pass is mine."

The bell rang. I put my joke list in my backpack, walked into class and sat at my desk.

Unfortunately, my desk was right next to Ajay's desk. Ajay glared at me.

I glared right back at him. He had no reason to be mad at me. It wasn't my fault that Ajay had no talent and that I had a great act. Everyone would love my jokes. I would win the talent show and the homework pass. I wouldn't have to do the research report. I should feel so great.

But really, I felt lonely and sad.

10

EVIL AT THE LUNCH TABLE

At lunchtime that day, I sat across from Gabby. The canteen smelled like I felt – foul. "Puke-urritos are the worst school lunches ever," I told Gabby.

"You mean bean burritos," Gabby said.

"Ajay and I call them puke-urritos because they look and smell like puke. It's a joke," I explained. But I knew that if you have to explain a joke to people, they won't find it funny.

Gabby yawned in response.

If Ajay were here, he would have laughed. Also, I would have joked about the carrots served with the burritos. I would have said carrots should be called "care-nots", because no one cares about them. I bet he would have laughed at that too.

I watched Ajay as he sat across from Will Carelli. They were pretty far from my table. I couldn't help staring.

When Ajay saw me staring, he frowned at me. I turned away.

Gabby yawned again. She said, "I stayed up late last night practising my song for the talent show."

"I stayed up late too," I said. "I was working on my comedy act."

"It sounds like Brooke is doing a comedy act now." Gabby pointed at her. Brooke was sitting at the other end of the table from Ajay and Will. Tessa Lee, Darla Jones and Latasha Kennedy were sitting near her and laughing.

I looked at Ajay again. He was frowning at Will. The lunchroom was very loud, but I could hear Will yodelling again. Ugh.

"I think Brooke is telling jokes," Gabby said.

I looked at Brooke again. She was holding up a paper and reading from it. The girls near her laughed again.

"The last time I heard anyone laugh so much, it was right after you told a joke," Gabby said.

"I found some great new jokes," I said. "I'm keeping them secret until the talent show."

When Tessa, Darla and Latasha stopped laughing, Brooke looked down at the paper and read from it again. The girls laughed again.

"I never thought Brooke was funny," Gabby said.

"Me neither," I said. I wondered how Brooke had become so funny. Had she been reading joke books like I had? Had she written down jokes on a piece of paper like I had done?

Then I realized something: The piece of paper Brooke was holding was yellow like my list of jokes, and it was the same size. Had Brooke stolen my joke list from my backpack?

I stood up and hurried to Brooke's table.

Before I got there, I saw Ajay standing behind Brooke. He pointed to the piece of paper she had been reading and said, "You stole my friend's jokes!"

I was really upset about that. But I was also really happy that Ajay had called me his friend. I stood next to him and said, "Yeah, Brooke. You stole that list of jokes from my backpack!"

"You can't prove that," Brooke said. "Maybe the list fell from your backpack by accident. And maybe I just happened to pick it up."

"I don't believe you. You told people my new jokes that I was saving for the talent show!" I said.

Brooke smiled. "Those are good jokes. I'm going to

keep telling them to the kids at school. By the time you tell them at the talent show, they will be old jokes and no one will laugh at them."

Ajay tried to grab the joke list. Brooke pulled her hand away, knocking over her carton of milk. Milk spilled all over her sandwich and crisps.

"My lunch is ruined!" Brooke said.

"Oops." Ajay smiled.

I tried to grab the joke list but accidentally bumped the carton of milk onto Brooke's lap.

"My new skirt!" Brooke said. "There's milk all over it now."

"Oops." I smiled.

Brooke glared at me. "Shelby, you knocked over the carton of milk on purpose."

"I did not," I said. "But even if I did, you can't prove that. So don't cry over spilled milk."

"I don't cry. I get even." Brooke's eyes narrowed evilly.

She said, "I am going to win the talent show. I'll surprise everyone with a brand-new outfit. It's too bad you can't surprise anyone with brand-new jokes. Now I will wash the milk from my skirt." Brooke stood and headed to the toilets.

After she left, I told Ajay, "Thanks for sticking up for me. And for calling me your friend."

"You're welcome," he said.

I was glad Ajay and I were friends again. But now neither of us had a good act for the talent show.

BATTLE FOR THE BEDROOM

Ajay and I sat next to each other on the bus after school. Even though it was hot and stuffy inside and the bus smelled like sweat, I was happy to be sitting next to my friend again.

Ajay said, "We need to start researching our reports."

I sighed. "Researching and writing about someone famous sounds so boring. I wish I could win the talent contest and get a homework pass instead."

"I wish I had Stephen Curry's basketball talent," Ajay said. "I would shoot free throws onstage, make twenty in a row and win the talent contest. When it counts the most, Stephen Curry can make the game-winning shot."

"Tina Fey is like that too," I said. "If I had Tina Fey's talent, I would make up funny jokes really fast and win the talent contest."

"I should start writing down ideas for my report." Ajay leaned over, grabbed the backpack that rested between his legs, unzipped it, and took out a pen and notebook.

"What famous person are you going to write about?" I asked.

"I have no idea," Ajay said. "Stephen Curry probably would have finished his report by now. He's known for working hard."

I took out a pen and notebook from my backpack. "Tina Fey is known for working hard too. She writes, acts and is a mum to two girls."

"Stephen Curry has two daughters too," Ajay said.

I stared at my notebook and said, "I wish I knew who to write about."

"Me too," Ajay said.

"Or we could keep trying to win the talent contest. Tina Fey wouldn't have given up so fast," I said.

"Neither would Stephen Curry," Ajay said.

I started writing in my notebook, even though the bumpy bus ride made my writing even sloppier than usual. I wasn't working on my report. Instead, I was listing ideas for the talent show.

Ajay wrote down ideas too. Soon we shared ideas and came up with a good plan – a secret one.

A few minutes after the bus dropped us off, Ajay came to my house. He brought his books on magic tricks, puppetry, singing, dancing and Stephen Curry. More importantly, he also brought over iced sugar biscuits. We ate all the biscuits. We also ate some brownies my dad had made. Then we went into my bedroom.

Unfortunately it was my sister's bedroom too. Even more unfortunately, my sister was in the room. And even more unfortunately than that, she was taping a new picture of Dalton Dash to the wall by her bed. She said, "Isn't Dalton Dash the cutest singer ever?"

"No," I said. "We need to practise for the talent show in here."

"I need to look at my Dalton Dash pictures in here," Lila said. "Practise in another room."

I crossed my arms. "We need to stay here with the door closed. Otherwise, Coop will bother us and Mum will take a thousand pictures of us for her blog."

"No they won't," Lila said.

Just then Coop opened our bedroom door and said, "Play with me! Let's play tag or freeze tag or tunnel tag or turtle tag or elbow tag or toilet tag or—"

"Sorry," I interrupted him. "We're too busy to play tag with you."

Then Mum walked in with her camera. She took pictures of Coop, Lila, Ajay and me. I told Mum her blog readers must be tired of seeing so many pictures of us. That just made Mum take pictures of other stuff – the floor, the ceiling, the wardrobe door and about a thousand other things. She even took a picture of the picture of Dalton Dash.

Finally, Coop and Mum left. But Lila stayed, sitting on her bed and filing her fingernails.

"I told you Coop would bother us and Mum would take a thousand pictures for her blog," I said to Lila.

"I'm staying in our bedroom," Lila said.

"Fine," I said. "You can watch Ajay's puppet show again."

Lila frowned.

"You can also listen to me sing," Ajay said with a smile. "My singing talent is about the same as my talent with puppets."

"No thanks." Lila hurried out of the room.

Ajay and I laughed.

Then we spent hours and hours preparing for the talent show. We used some of the stuff from my joke books and Ajay's books on magic and puppetry. We also made up a lot of stuff on our own. We worked so hard, we didn't do any of our homework or start our research reports.

We really needed to win homework passes.

12

A PIRATE, A SCARECROW AND A COW

At break time the next day, Ajay and I queued up for the handball court. Only two people could play at a time, so there was a long queue. I loved smashing the ball against the wall with my fists and trying to get the ball after the other player had smashed it against the wall. So it was worth waiting for.

"Shelby," Jack Lopez said. He was standing in front of me in the queue. He turned to me and said, "I know you like jokes. Here's a good one: What's a pirate's favourite letter?"

"Arrr," I said like a pirate. "I was going to tell that joke at the talent show. Where did you hear it?"

"Brooke Crumpkin told me," he said. "She's really funny."

Brooke was only funny because she had stolen my pirate joke. I wished I could make Brooke walk the plank.

Tessa Lee got in the queue behind Ajay. She said, "Why did the scarecrow win a prize?"

"Because he was outstanding in his field," Jack said. "Brooke told me that one yesterday."

"She told it to me this morning," Tessa said.

That was another joke Brooke had stolen from me. I wished I could make her stand in a field.

Brooke walked over and asked, "Why do cows jump on trampolines?"

"So they can make milkshakes," I said.

Jack and Tessa laughed as we moved forward in the handball queue.

"Speaking of cows," I said, "joke stealers put me in a bad mooood."

Jack and Tessa laughed again.

Brooke snobbishly raised her nose in the air. "You can't prove I stole jokes from you, Shelby," she said. "By the way, I told those jokes to a lot of people."

"You're a joke thief," Ajay said.

"Ajay, you have no talent," Brooke said. "You dance like a clown, you sing like a fire alarm and you play basketball like a toddler."

"Brooke, the only talents you have are for being mean and for having the world's biggest bogey in your nose," I said.

She gasped and cupped her hand over her nose. Then she stomped away.

Maybe I couldn't prove Brooke had stolen my list of jokes, but I could get back at her. Now that I had planned my new talent show act, I could start planning my revenge on Brooke.

But first it was finally my turn to play handball. Jack hit the ball against the wall. I let it bounce once and then took out my anger on the ball, hitting it with all my might. It bounced off the wall really hard and really fast before going far out of bounds.

13

BIG NIGHT AND BIG REVENGE

On the night of the talent show, I got to the school hall early with my family. We sat in the front row. I put the large plastic bag I had brought under my seat. I had told my parents I needed extra time to set up. I hadn't told them I needed to set up Brooke for failure.

Ajay got to the hall early too, just as we had planned. He was carrying a large plastic bag.

"Have your brought your props?" I whispered as Ajay sat in the row behind me.

Ajay nodded. "Are you nervous about going onstage?" he asked.

"No," I replied. I had worked hard on my new act and practised it about a thousand times. There was nothing to be nervous about.

I stared at the entrance of the hall. Latasha and her family came in and sat next to my family in the front row. Latasha's mother said, "Latasha, I hope you do well tonight. But even if you don't, I'm proud that you're performing."

Darla Jones and her mother sat in the second row. Darla's mother said, "You had better win, Darla. Win, win, win! I will be upset if you don't win first place."

Jack Lopez and his parents sat in the third row. Jack's parents didn't say anything. They were staring at their phones.

Then Brooke and her parents came and stood in the aisle. Each of Brooke's parents carried a large shopping bag. Brooke's father said, "Brooke, we know you're the most talented person ever."

Her mother said, "Brooke, we know you're a total winner. If you don't win first place, it's not your fault."

"I know," Brooke said. "Now go backstage and hang up my gorgeous outfit. Make sure my dress doesn't get wrinkled. It needs to stay perfect."

Her parents carried the large bags backstage.

Ajay and I followed them backstage, just as we had planned. Well, we had planned to follow them quietly, but Ajay sneezed loudly. I tried to whisper, "Gesundheit", but it came out almost as loud as Ajay's sneeze.

Luckily, Brooke's parents didn't seem to notice us. They were busy talking. Brooke's mother said, "She is so lovely."

Her father said, "She's such a sweet girl."

"They can't be talking about Brooke," Ajay whispered to me.

"Yeah. Brooke isn't lovely or sweet," I whispered back.

Brooke's parents hung her new dress on a hanger from a hook on the wall. The dress was purple and silky, with shiny gold ruffles on the ends of the long sleeves and around the bottom hem. It didn't seem that great to me, but I didn't know much about fashion.

Brooke's parents carefully placed her new tights and boots against the wall. Finally, they took their seats next to their not-so-lovely and not-so-sweet daughter.

As soon as they left, Ajay and I got to work. It took us only a few minutes to carry out our plan of revenge. When we returned to our seats, Ms Fish was walking onstage. She said loudly, "Everyone, please sit down. The talent show will begin in one minute."

"Are you nervous?" Ajay asked again.

I shook my head. "Not at all." Yesterday, Ms Fish

had told us the order of the acts. So I knew I wouldn't be going onstage for a while.

I stared at the stage and thought about my favourite comedian, Tina Fey. She had performed in shows when she was a kid. I wondered if anyone had ever stolen her jokes. I hoped I could be as funny and famous as her one day.

From my front row seat, I turned and stared at the audience. Everyone in my class and their friends and family were here tonight – probably close to a hundred people. I suddenly felt nervous.

I took a big gulp of air. I wondered if Tina Fey ever got nervous before performing. Did her cheeks get warm? Mine did. Did she feel like a rotten egg was rolling around in her stomach? I did. Did her throat get dry? Mine did.

I gulped again, but that didn't help my nerves.

Ms Fish clapped her hands three times. All the kids knew that meant to be quiet, so we stopped talking. But it took the grown-ups longer to be quiet.

Finally everyone was quiet, except for Latasha's mother. She told Latasha's father, "Don't tell anyone, but I think talent shows are really boring."

The audience laughed.

Latasha's mum put her head down and said, "I'm so embarrassed!"

Once the laughter stopped, Ms Fish said, "Good evening. Welcome to our class talent show. Many of the pupils will perform tonight. I will announce the winner after the last act."

Everyone clapped.

"The children have been working hard. I know they are eager to perform," Ms Fish said.

I had been working hard. I had been eager to perform. But I wasn't anymore. I doubted I could even get onstage. I was much too nervous.

14

BURP, YODEL, SPLAT

"Let's all clap for our first performer, Nick Sparangus," Ms Fish said.

Everyone clapped. Nick walked to the centre of the stage. Ms Fish moved to the side of the stage.

Beautiful violin music started playing. Nick opened his mouth and let out a big burp. Then he burped again. He kept burping to the beat of the music. He was very talented at burping. He was also very disgusting.

My parents frowned. My sister shook her head. Ms Fish, who was judging the talent show, frowned and shook her head. My little brother smiled. I smiled too, because I knew Nick wouldn't win the talent show. When Nick finished, he took a deep bow and let out a final burp. Most of the audience, including Nick's parents, clapped very quietly.

My little brother clapped long and hard. He said, "I want to learn how to burp like that!"

My parents frowned even more.

Will Carelli walked onstage next. He wore a polo shirt, shorts and braces. He stood in the middle of the stage, cupped his hands around his mouth, and yodelled. *"Yodel – Ay – Eee – Oooo! Yodel – Ay – Eee – Oooo! Yodel – Ay – Eee – Oooo!"* He yodelled like that about a thousand times. It seemed to take a thousand hours.

Ms Fish walked over to him and said, "Thank you, Will."

He yodelled again: *"Yodel – Ay – Eee – Oooo!"*

"That's enough, Will," Ms Fish said.

He said, *"Yodel – Ay – Eee – Oooo!"* one more time. Then he took a deep, long bow.

Will got even less applause than Nick had got for his burping. But Will's mother clapped very loudly and said, "Wonderful! Just wonderful!"

My parents frowned again, my sister shook her head again and Coop and I smiled again.

Coop said, "This is the best show ever! I want to learn how to yodel too."

My mum whispered to my dad, "What's next? Farting in tune?"

"I hope so!" Coop said.

Ms Fish announced that Alice would perform a ballet dance next. I didn't think ballet dancing involved farting – at least not on purpose.

Alice stood at the back of the stage. She wore a white leotard, white tights, a bright pink tutu and soft pink ballet slippers. Pretty piano music started playing. Alice ran on tiptoes to the front of the stage. She kept her legs straight, her arms reaching above her head and her fingertips touching each other. Then she spun in circles.

"That's beautiful," my sister said.

Alice spun and spun.

"She's very talented," my mother whispered as Alice kept spinning.

Alice's legs started to wobble. Her arms dropped to her sides. She said, "I'm dizzy." Then she fell to the floor.

Ms Fish hurried to Alice and asked her, "Are you OK?"

Alice nodded and repeated, "I'm dizzy."

Ms Fish helped Alice stand up.

Alice said, "I think I did too many spins. I'm OK now, but I'm dizzy."

Then Ms Fish walked Alice offstage. Alice's parents put their arms around her and guided her to her seat.

Ms Fish returned to the stage and said, "Let's give Alice a big hand."

The audience clapped a lot harder for Alice's dizzy dancing than they did for Nick's burping or Will's yodelling.

Then Ms Fish said, "Latasha Kennedy will now show us her gymnastics talent."

"Time to go backstage," Ajay whispered to me.

Ack! It was almost my turn to perform. I was supposed to go onstage after Latasha's gymnastics and Darla's violin acts. Watching the talent show the past few minutes had made me forget to be nervous. But now I was nervous all over again.

A MOB OF MAD MIAOWS

I needed to go backstage to get ready, so I stood up. My legs were shaking so much they barely held up my body. Also, my cheeks were burning, my stomach felt like a boulder was rolling inside it and the inside of my mouth seemed as dry as a desert. I couldn't perform my act like this. My legs were shaking so much, it took me a long time to get backstage.

Ajay was already there, standing next to the large bag he had brought. He said, "Shelby, you look a bit nervous."

"I'm not a bit nervous," I said. "I'm a *lot* nervous."

"Did Tina Fey ever get nervous before she went onstage?" Ajay asked.

"Many times," I said.

"Did Tina Fey ever perform really badly?" Ajay asked.

I nodded. "She made a lot of mistakes when she was starting out."

"Think about that," Ajay said.

I did. Tina Fey had gone onstage even when she was nervous and even after she had made mistakes. Tina Fey never gave up.

"I'm not giving up. I'm going onstage," I said. As I thought about Tina Fey, my legs got less shaky. My cheeks cooled down a little. My stomach felt less queasy. My mouth didn't feel so dry.

I heard the audience clapping. Latasha must have finished her gymnastics routine.

I heard Ms Fish say, "Now Darla Jones will play the violin."

I told Ajay, "I didn't know Darla could play the violin."

Suddenly it sounded as if a large mob of angry cats had invaded the stage.

Ajay said, "The reason you didn't know Darla could play the violin is because Darla *can't* play the violin."

I covered my ears and nodded. After about a thousand minutes of listening to a large mob of angry cats, the audience clapped.

"I bet they're clapping from relief that Darla stopped playing her violin," I said.

"Ready?" Ajay asked.

I nodded, even though I still felt pretty nervous.

"Now please welcome Shelby Bloom, who will be performing comedy," Ms Fish said. "Joining her onstage is Ajay Patel. They call their act Bloom-Patel LOL."

16

BLOOM-PATEL
LOL

I started from the right side of the stage and ran towards the middle. Ajay started from the left side and ran towards the middle. We each carried a bag of props.

We reached centre stage at the same time and pretended to crash into each other. Then we pretended to bounce off of each other and fall back. We both landed on our bottoms. The audience laughed.

Brooke said loudly from her seat, "That's not funny."

My little brother shouted, "Yes it is!"

Ajay and I stood up. Ajay said, "Falling on our bottoms is just one of our many talents. We also do magic." He took a pack of cards from his bag and said, "Shelby, pick a card. Show the card to the audience, but don't show me."

"Ajay also has a great talent for being bossy," I joked.

The audience laughed.

Brooke let out a loud fake yawn.

I took a card from the middle of the pack and showed it to the audience.

"Now put the card back in the pack," Ajay said.

"You're not the boss of me!" I shouted, pretending to be mad.

The audience laughed.

Ajay pointed at me and then tapped his finger on the pack of cards.

I put my card back in the pack and said, "I guess you are the boss of me."

The audience laughed again.

Brooke faked another loud yawn.

"Get ready for some magic," Ajay said. "The card Shelby chose will fly through the air. Abracadabra, blabra, shmabra."

Ajay threw the entire pack of cards in the air. He said, "Shelby's card is in there somewhere."

The audience laughed again.

I crossed my arms and pretended to pout. It was hard to act mad, because I was so happy our act was getting laughs.

"Boring," Brooke said.

"No it's not!" my little brother shouted.

I tried to ignore them. I pulled out a basketball from my bag and said, "You'll be amazed at my ball-handling skills. I'm really fast." I dribbled the ball in place for a few seconds.

Ajay pretended to try to steal the basketball.

I picked up the ball, clutched it against my chest and

ran across the stage. Then I said, "I told you I'm really fast."

"Amazing," Ajay said.

The audience laughed.

Brooke didn't make any rude comments this time. I saw Ms Fish talking to her. Both of them were frowning. I hoped Brooke was getting a big punishment.

Next Ajay and I stood on opposite sides of the stage. I held the basketball, and Ajay held a hoop.

Ajay said, "Shelby can throw the ball all the way into this hoop. Let's count down." He led the audience in a countdown: "Ten. Nine. Eight . . ." With each number, Ajay and I moved closer to each other.

When the countdown reached "One", Ajay and I stood only a short distance apart. I dropped the ball through the hoop.

The audience laughed.

"I am a great ventriloquist," Ajay said. He stood behind me, put his hand on my back and said, "This is Shelby. Shelby is my dummy."

"I prefer the word *puppet*," I said, moving my mouth and keeping the rest of my body still. "This is Ajay. Ajay is annoying."

"That's not nice," Ajay said. "Apologize."

"OK. I'm sorry you're annoying," I said.

The audience laughed.

Brooke said, "I don't get it."

Tessa Lee said, "Shelby's pretending to be Ajay's puppet."

Ms Fish said, "Shhh."

"Do you know what's even more annoying?" I said, still acting like a puppet, with my mouth moving and my body still.

"Brooke Crumpkin stealing all the jokes you were going to use for this talent show?" Ajay asked.

Some people in the audience gasped.

Brooke said, "You can't prove that."

I said, "When Brooke stole my jokes, it was very

annoying. But now the puppet show is over, and it's time for some knock-knock jokes. **Knock, knock.**"

"Who's there?" Ajay asked.

"Yeah," I said.

Ajay pointed to the audience. They all asked, "Yeah who?"

"Yahoo! This talent show is exciting!" I said.

I heard laughs, giggles, a few groans and a woman say, "Did Brooke really steal her jokes?"

I said, "Knock, knock" again.

"Who's there?" Ajay and the audience asked.

"Impatient cow," I said.

"Impatient c—"

I interrupted them. "Mooooo!"

That joke got a lot of laughs.

"Knock, knock," I said.

"Who's there?" Ajay and the audience asked.

"Toodle," I said.

"Toodle who?" the audience asked.

Ajay and I said together, "Toodle-oo and goodbye!"

Then we bowed very low and fell to the floor, just as we had planned.

A second later, we jumped up, waved at the audience and ran off the stage together.

We got very loud applause. When I got back to my seat, my parents were still laughing.

My brother said, "You guys were almost as good as the burping guy."

Even my sister said, "Good job."

I was pretty sure Ajay and I had just won homework passes. And I was glad we had told everyone about Brooke being a joke stealer.

17

A THOUSAND HOURS LATER

Ms Fish said, "There are only three more performers: Gabby Garcia, Jessica Cho and Brooke Crumpkin. Let's welcome Gabby to the stage."

As the audience clapped, Brooke went backstage to put on her modelling outfit.

I turned around and winked at Ajay.

Ajay winked back at me.

Gabby walked to a piano near the front of the stage. She wore a bright red dress with frills on the shoulders.

Piano music played. Gabby began singing sweetly. She sang, "I loved you, but I lost you. Oh, oh, oh." When she sang the "Oh, oh, oh" part, she sounded truly sad. She sang about a dog searching for his owner every day and howling at the moon every night. "I loved you, but I lost you. Oh, oh, oh."

My eyes got watery.

Gabby sang about a tiny, hopeful seed straining to sprout in the dry desert. Then she sang the chorus, "I loved you, but I lost you. Oh, oh, oh."

I started sniffling.

Gabby sang about grey clouds that looked like broken hearts. "I loved you, but I lost you. Oh, oh, oh."

A few tears ran down my cheeks.

I looked around. Mum was wiping a tear from her eye. Ajay was sniffling. Dad had tears streaming down his cheeks. Everyone sitting near me was so sad – except for

Coop, who was playing a game on Mum's mobile phone.

By the end of the song, Gabby was crying a little too.

The audience clapped and sniffled and clapped some more.

Ms Fish came onstage. Wiping away a tear, she said, "What a beautiful—"

"Ack!" Brooke's angry voice came from backstage. "Who did this?"

"What's going on?" Ms Fish asked.

Ajay and I smiled at each other, even though both of us were still crying a little. We did not tell Ms Fish what was going on.

Jessica walked onstage next. Holding a piece of paper, she said, "I will read a poem I wrote all by myself." She looked down at the paper and read:

I like trees.

You see.

I also like cheese.

If it's Swiss cheese.

I don't like goat's cheese.

Or strong cheddar cheese.

But I like mild cheddar cheese.

And grilled cheese.

And macaroni and cheese.

I covered my mouth and yawned.

"Ack!" Brooke yelled again backstage. "No!"

Jessica kept reading her poem.

I don't like fleas.

Or peas. But I like peace.

And the police.

"This is boring," Coop whispered.

"Shhh," Mum said.

"I like poems," Dad said.

Jessica kept reading her poem.

And I like geese.

Except for mean geese.

I like nice geese.

I don't like to freeze.

Or bees.

I like the letter B.

But not the insects called bees.

Or being teased.

I fell asleep.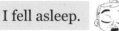

I woke up a few minutes later. My brother and sister had fallen asleep.

Jessica was still reading her poem:

Also, I don't like disease.

Like kidney disease.

Or Lyme disease.

I really don't like any disease.

Or a sneeze.

Or a wheeze.

Or grazed knees.

I don't know if I like Louise.

Because I don't know anyone called Louise.

Finally, after about a thousand hours, Jessica said, "The end, if you please."

She didn't get much applause. Most of the audience was asleep. My dad said, "I like poems," again.

Ms Fish returned to the stage and said, "And now our last performer, Brooke Crumpkin. She will be modelling an outfit and talking about fashion."

KNOTTY DEEDS

Brooke slowly walked onstage in her new dress. She was scowling and carrying a round, gold object in her arms. She said loudly, "I'm very mad!"

Everyone in the audience woke up.

"I was going to model my most beautiful outfit, but someone ruined it," Brooke said. "My gold tights are knotted up into a ball."

She held up the round gold object and said, "Tights are not supposed to look like balls."

Then Brooke bent down and pointed to her boots. "Someone tied the laces of my boots together in another bunch of knots. That's why I walked onstage so slowly. My boots are tied together."

Ms Fish hurried onstage and put her arm around Brooke. Then she started sniffing and said, "Something smells funny."

"My boots smell funny," Brooke said. "Someone stuffed them with tuna."

"I'm sorry this happened," Ms Fish said.

"You know who's not sorry?" Brooke pointed at me. "Shelby Bloom is not sorry. She's the one who did all this."

The audience gasped.

"How do you know Shelby did it?" Ms Fish asked.

"Because she's mad I stole her jokes," Brooke said.

I stood and said, "You finally admitted you stole my new jokes and ruined the act I was going to perform."

Brooke crossed her arms. "You ruined my act by messing up my new outfit."

I crossed my arms. "You can't prove that."

"I bet your friend Ajay helped you mess up my outfit," Brooke said.

"Let's discuss this later," Ms Fish said. "Brooke, are you going to perform your act?"

"No!" she shouted.

"Then please leave the stage," Ms Fish said. "It's getting late, and I need to announce the winner of the talent show."

A WHOLE LOT OF SORRIES

After Brooke left the stage and the audience were quiet, it was finally time for Ms Fish to announce the winner of the talent contest.

I turned and whispered to Ajay, "I'm sure we've won."

Ms Fish said, "The winner of the talent contest – and the homework pass – had a very entertaining act."

"That's us," I whispered to Ajay.

"The act was a huge hit with the audience," Ms Fish said.

"That is definitely us," I said. I stood up.

Ms Fish said, "The winner of the talent show is Latasha Kennedy for her fantastic gymnastics act."

I groaned and sat down.

Ajay groaned behind me.

Latasha left her seat and made her way to Ms Fish. She did three amazing flips and a great walking handstand along the way. She was an excellent gymnast.

Ms Fish handed Latasha the homework pass and said, "Thank you to all the performers and everyone in our audience. Good night." Then Ms Fish frowned and said, "Brooke, Ajay and Shelby, please come up here with your parents."

I looked at Ajay and raised my eyebrows. I had a headache.

Ajay rubbed his forehead as if he had a headache too.

Mum said, "Shelby, you shouldn't have ruined Brooke Crumpkin's outfit. You're grounded. You will stay in the house all weekend."

Ajay's dad said, "You too, Ajay."

Ms Fish also punished us. On the bright side, she punished Brooke too. This is what we had to do:

Brooke, Ajay and I had to stay after school every day for a week.

Brooke had to apologize to me for stealing my jokes.

Brooke had to apologize to Ajay for insulting him.

Ajay and I had to tell Brooke we were sorry for spilling her milk and messing up her modelling outfit.

Ajay and I had to untie all the knots on Brooke's tights and boot laces and clean the tuna from her boots.

We all had to complete our missing homework.

We all had to work on our research reports.

Ajay ended up writing his report on his hero, Stephen Curry. I wrote my report on my hero, Tina Fey. We learned a lot of interesting things about them.

Brooke did her report on a boring fashion model. She learned a lot of boring things about her hero.

I had fun reading jokes by Tina Fey while I researched my report. I wrote down Tina Fey's best jokes, in case there was another talent show. If there was, I wanted to team up with Ajay again.

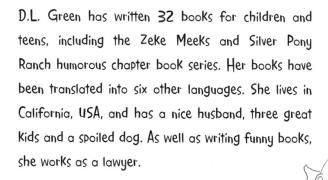

D.L. Green has written 32 books for children and teens, including the Zeke Meeks and Silver Pony Ranch humorous chapter book series. Her books have been translated into six other languages. She lives in California, USA, and has a nice husband, three great kids and a spoiled dog. As well as writing funny books, she works as a lawyer.

Illustrator Leandra La Rosa lives and works in Palermo, Sicily. She was born in Trapani, a town on the island's western side, and since childhood her main interests have been illustration, animation and music. Leandra studied at the Academy of Fine Arts in Palermo and obtained a degree in graphic design. Since 2013 she has been working as a graphic designer and illustrator for many Italian agencies and publishing houses.

READ THEM ALL!

The Funny Girl — Good Deeds and Other Laughing Matters

The Funny Girl — Making Friends and Horsing Around

The Funny Girl — Something Smells Funny at the Talent Show

The Funny Girl — Being a Punch Line Is No Joke